Jessica

the Jazz
Fairy

by Daisy Meadows

SCHOLASTIC INC.

New York   Toronto   London   Auckland   Sydney
Mexico City   New Delhi   Hong Kong   Buenos Aires

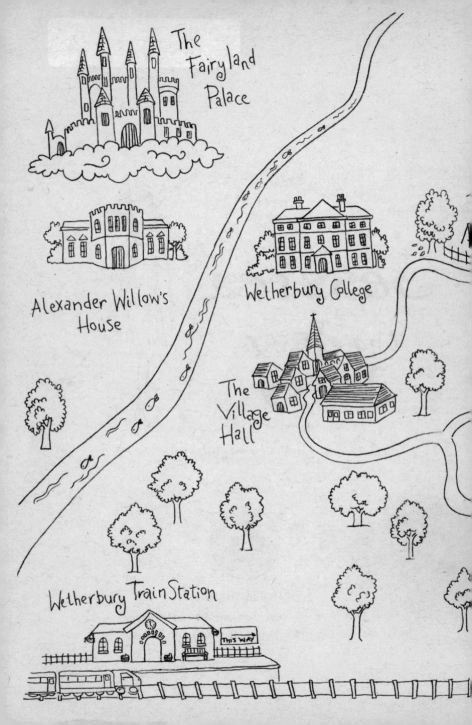

The Fairyland Palace

Alexander Willow's House

Wetherbury College

The Village Hall

Wetherbury Train Station

THIS WAY

Jessica
the Jazz
Fairy

To Remy Smet,

keep on dancing

Special thanks to Narinder Dhami

No part of this work may be reproduced, stored in a retrieval system,
or transmitted in any form or by any means, electronic, mechanical,
photocopying, recording, or otherwise, without written permission
of the publisher. For information regarding permission, write to
Rainbow Magic Limited c/o HIT Entertainment,
830 South Greenville Avenue, Allen, TX 75002-3320.

ISBN-10: 0-545-10621-4
ISBN-13: 978-0-545-10621-4

12 11 10 9 8 7 6 5 4   11 12 13/0

Printed in the U.S.A.

First Scholastic Printing, May 2009

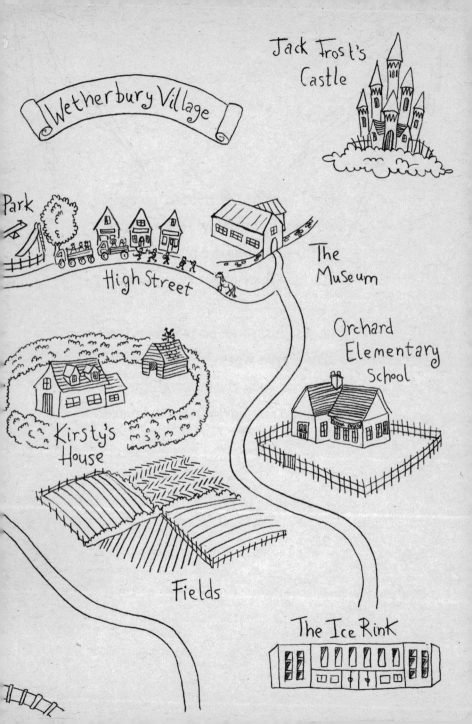

Hold tight to the ribbons, please.
You goblins may now feel a breeze.
I'm summoning a hurricane
To take the ribbons away again.

But, goblins, you'll be swept up too,
For I have work for you to do.
Guard each ribbon carefully,
By using your new power to freeze.

Contents

Jessica Makes an Entrance

"I'm sooo excited!" Kirsty Tate said
happily, as she smoothed down the satin
skirt of her long purple dress. "I've never
been to a grown-up party before!"

"Me neither," Rachel Walker, Kirsty's
best friend, agreed. Like Kirsty, she was
dressed in a brand-new outfit, a floaty

cream-colored dress with sequins around the hem and neckline. Along with Kirsty's parents, the girls were on their way to a party at the home of Alexander Willow, a friend of Mr. and Mrs. Tate.

"It's not far now," Mr. Tate replied, steering the car down a dark, narrow country lane. "You're going to have a great time, girls. Alexander's a producer of Broadway musicals, and he always throws *wonderful* parties!"

"There's going to be a jazz band and lots of dancing!" added Mrs. Tate.

In the back of the car, Kirsty and Rachel exchanged a knowing glance. While Rachel was staying with Kirsty over their school vacation, the two girls had been helping their very special friends, the Dance Fairies. The fairies' magic dance ribbons were missing. The ribbons were very important because their magic helped make dancing fun, in both Fairyland and the human world. The ribbons also made sure that dance performances went well. But Jack Frost had stolen the ribbons. He wanted their magic powers to help his goblins learn to dance.

When the king and queen of Fairyland
had demanded that the ribbons be
returned to the Dance Fairies, Jack Frost
cast an icy spell that sent seven of his
goblins tumbling into the
human world. Each
goblin clutched one of
the magic ribbons.
The goblins were
supposed to keep the
ribbons hidden, but so
far Kirsty and Rachel,
with the help of the
Dance Fairies, had
managed to get four of them back.

"Jessica the Jazz Fairy's ribbon is still
missing," Kirsty whispered eagerly.
"Maybe the goblin who has her ribbon
will be at the party tonight!"

Rachel nodded. The girls knew that the magical ribbon was drawn to its own type of dance. "I hope so, too, Kirsty," Rachel whispered. "We have to get the ribbon back, or else the party will be ruined!"

"What kind of dancing will there be, Mom?" Kirsty asked as Mr. Tate drove between two iron gates and up a long, winding driveway. "Rachel and I don't really know what jazz dance is!"

Mrs. Tate nodded. "Jazz music is very modern, and so is jazz dance," she explained. "You've probably both seen lots of jazz dancing in musicals."

"Oh, great!" Rachel exclaimed happily, "I *love* that kind of dancing!"

Kirsty stared out of the car window, her eyes wide. "I've never seen such an *enormous* garden!" she said. "Rachel, look at that pond with the mermaid fountain in the middle."

Rachel gazed out the window. "And *look* at the house!" she added, pointing.

The manor house in front of them was huge and looked very old. Its stone front was beautiful and impressive, with lots of windows and a large wooden door.

Rows of cars were already parked outside, and people were climbing out of them. The women were dressed in long, elegant ballgowns in a rainbow of colors, and the men all wore tuxedos and stylish suits.

As they entered the hall of the manor, the girls looked around eagerly. The house was lit by tall white candles. The flickering flames filled the hall with a warm yellow glow. Golden chocolate

coins had been scattered over
the antique tables, and
large gold platters
piled high with
cupcakes had
been placed
here and
there.

"Oh, this
is *gorgeous!*"
Kirsty
sighed.

Everyone
else was
making their
way through
the house toward the
back garden, so
the Tates and Rachel followed.

The garden was even more spectacular than the house. Kirsty and Rachel stared open-mouthed as they walked past exotic plants in huge china pots, a rippling turquoise swimming pool, and an intricate maze made of neatly trimmed hedges. A white tent had been set up in the middle of the garden for the party.

As the girls walked in, they could see gold stars sparkling from the ceiling of the tent. Tables and chairs had been set up for the guests. A jazz band sat on a stage at the back, playing a catchy tune that quickly had Kirsty and Rachel tapping their toes.

"Nobody's dancing yet, thank goodness!" Rachel whispered, noting the

empty dance floor in the middle of
the tent.

"Everyone's too busy eating and
talking," Kirsty whispered back,
watching the waiters who were carrying
trays of drinks and offering them to the
guests. "But there are lots of places for a
goblin to hide!"

Rachel nodded. "We'll just have to

keep looking," she said determinedly, scanning the party tent.

"That's Alexander over there, girls," said Mrs. Tate, pointing to a tall, blond man who was chatting with other guests. "We'll introduce you later, but I can tell you want to explore. Why don't you go and have a look around now?"

"Thanks, Mom," Kirsty said. She and Rachel wandered off, winding between the chairs and tables. "Would you like a fruit juice cocktail, girls?" asked a waiter. He was holding a tray that had two tall crystal glasses on top, decorated with pretty paper umbrellas. "They're delicious."

"Yes, please!" Kirsty and Rachel said at the same time, each taking one of the glasses.

Rachel took a sip. "Yum!" she exclaimed as the waiter hurried off. "It *is* delicious!"

Kirsty raised the glass to her lips to take a sip herself. But then she gasped aloud. There, sitting on the rim of the crystal glass, twirling the umbrella and smiling up at her, was Jessica the Jazz Fairy!

Enter the Goblin

"Rachel, look!" Kirsty laughed as Jessica rose to her feet, still holding the umbrella. Balancing daintily on the edge of the glass, the tiny fairy waved up at the girls. She wore a silky pink dress with a deeper pink sash and a matching long, pink feather boa around her neck. High-heeled silver shoes sparkled on her

feet, and golden curls tumbled down
her back.

"Hello, girls," Jessica called softly,
putting down the umbrella. "I've come
to find my ribbon!"

Quickly, Kirsty and Rachel hurried
over to a quiet corner of the tent, away

from the other guests.
Jessica took a cautious
look around, then
fluttered from the glass
onto Kirsty's shoulder.
"Is your ribbon here,
Jessica?" Rachel
asked eagerly.

Jessica nodded. "I'm sure it is!" she
replied. "The magic of my ribbon
probably brought the goblin here, since
the party has a jazz theme!"

"Ladies and gentlemen!" came a loud announcement from the stage, making Rachel and Kirsty jump.

The girls turned to see what was going on. The saxophone player from the jazz band had stepped up to the microphone and was grinning at the audience.

"As a special birthday present for Alexander, the cast of his new musical, *Jazz It Up!* is going to perform a number from the show — just for him!" the musician explained.

The guests broke into applause and cheers. Alexander Willow looked surprised, but happy.

"Oh, this is going to be a disaster without Jessica's magic ribbon!" Rachel said anxiously, as the dancers ran onto the stage to more applause. The women were dressed in short sequined skirts and vests while the men wore black pants, white shirts, and silk scarves knotted around their necks. They all had sparkling top hats on their heads.

Jessica looked very sad.

"This would be an amazing performance if only the jazz ribbon was in its proper place on my wand!" She sighed heavily.

The jazz band struck an upbeat tune as the dancers quickly took their places. They began to strut across the stage, throwing their arms up into the air in sequence and singing,

Jazz it up!
Join us tonight and
Jazz it up!

"I can't watch!" Rachel groaned, covering her eyes with her hands.

Kirsty knew exactly how Rachel felt, but she forced herself to keep looking. The men and women had separated into two groups, still singing along to the music as they began to dance.

"Those are fantastic fan kicks," Jessica murmured approvingly as the women high-kicked their way across the stage.

"And those barrel jumps and hip rolls are right in time with the music."

Kirsty watched curiously as the male dancers performed split jumps and the women danced around them. They were all doing really well, and nothing had gone wrong yet!

"Rachel?" Kirsty nudged her friend. "It's OK. Their number is going fabulously!"

"Oh!" Rachel peeked through her fingers and then smiled at Kirsty. "But that means . . ."

"My ribbon must be very close by!" Jessica chimed in excitedly.

Kirsty nodded, searching the stage for a goblin or the magic ribbon. At first, she didn't see anything out of the ordinary. But suddenly, her gaze was drawn to one of the dancers at the back. He was smaller than the others and it seemed strange that his silk scarf was tied around his face instead of his neck. He appeared to be the best dancer on the stage. "Look!" Kirsty said, pointing him out to Rachel and Jessica as the dancers did a final spin. "There's something kind of funny about that dancer, isn't there?"

Jessica frowned as she watched. The dancers were now lifting off their top hats and passing them down the line to the next person as they crossed the stage, but the smallest dancer refused to take his hat off. It clearly annoyed the girl behind him.

At that moment, Kirsty and Rachel both noticed that, unlike the others, the smallest dancer had a pink silk ribbon tied around his top hat.

"I recognize that ribbon!" Jessica announced, her voice trembling with excitement. "That dancer is a goblin in disguise — and he has my magic jazz ribbon!"

Goblin Takes a Bow

"That explains why he was dancing so well — and why the others were, too!" Rachel exclaimed as the music finished. The dancers all took their bows to loud applause.

"Let's follow the dancers as they come offstage. We can try to get the ribbon back," Kirsty suggested.

The audience was still applauding, so the dancers took a second bow.

"They were amazing, weren't they?" said a woman at a table near Rachel and Kirsty. "I can't wait to see the show on Broadway!"

"And wasn't that young boy at the back excellent?" her friend remarked.

"Luckily, nobody realizes he was a goblin," Rachel whispered to Kirsty, looking relieved.

"We'd better hurry backstage," Kirsty replied. "We might get a chance to grab the ribbon as the goblin comes offstage."

Jessica quickly ducked out of sight behind Kirsty's hair and the two girls headed backstage. There, they quickly hid behind a rack of costumes near the wings. The three friends watched the dancers walking offstage.

The goblin was last in the line. But instead of following the other dancers, he hurried to the front of the stage and took another

bow on his own, carefully holding the top hat on his head. The audience laughed and continued to clap. The goblin made another sweeping bow, still

 holding on to the top hat. This time, he bent over so low that the hat almost touched the ground. "He's having too much fun to leave the stage!" Kirsty laughed. The goblin waved graciously at the audience and bowed a third time.

The girls watched in amusement as the saxophone player went over to the goblin and took his arm.

The goblin pulled himself free, skipped

over to the side of the stage, and bowed
again. The saxophone player frowned
and hurried after the goblin, but the
goblin managed to dodge him and run to
the *other* side of the stage. The audience
was now in fits of laughter.

"They think it's all part of the show!"
Rachel whispered.

At last, the saxophone player managed
to grab the goblin's arm and march
him away.

"Remember that the goblin has the freezing power Jack Frost gave him," Jessica reminded Rachel and Kirsty. "So don't get too close to him."

The girls carefully peeked around the rack of costumes as the goblin finally came offstage. He hummed and skipped along happily, very proud of himself. But then he stopped suddenly. He pulled his silk scarf away from his face slightly and revealed a long, green, pointy nose. In fact, it was the longest, pointiest goblin nose Rachel had ever seen!

She glanced at Kirsty and could tell
that her friend was thinking exactly the
same thing. None of the goblins had *small*
noses, but this one was huge!

The goblin sniffed the air cautiously.
Then he sniffed again, so hard that
Rachel could see his nostrils quivering.
To her horror, he spun around and
walked toward the rack of costumes.

"I think the goblin sniffed us out!"
Rachel whispered nervously to Kirsty
and Jessica. "He's coming straight
toward us!"

Kitchen Chaos

"We have to do something!" Kirsty whispered.

"I'll turn you into fairies right now!" Jessica said quickly. "Then we'll be able to fly away if the goblin spots us."

She waved her wand and deep pink sparkles floated down around Rachel

and Kirsty, shrinking them right where they stood. Glittery, glimmering fairy wings appeared on their backs, and the two girls smiled with delight. They'd been fairies many times before, but it was *always* so much fun.

"Now stay as still as you can!" Jessica said softly.

All three of them held their breath as they waited for the goblin to pull the rack of costumes aside and find them. But nothing happened. Confused, Rachel, Kirsty, and Jessica peeked out again, just in time to see the goblin disappearing through the exit in front of their hiding place.

"He's going outside," Rachel whispered with a sigh of relief.

"We'd better follow him!" said Jessica.

But as they zoomed after the goblin, they heard the band strike up another melody.

"I think the dancing's starting," Kirsty pointed out.

"Then we have to get the ribbon back fast, or it will be a disaster!" Jessica said firmly. "Follow that goblin, girls!"

Jessica and the girls flew out the exit and after the goblin. He was hurrying across the garden toward the manor.

The three friends followed him into the
house. Once inside, he stopped, pulled
down his scarf, and sniffed the air again.
Then he raced off down a long, twisting
hallway.

"He can smell *something*!" Jessica
whispered, as they flew after him. "But
what?"

Ahead of them, the goblin had stopped
in an open doorway. He was now
sniffing the air very hard, with a look of
delight on his face.

"I can smell it now, too. It's fresh–
baked brownies," Kirsty said. "We must
be near the kitchen."

Jessica and the girls flew down the hall
and hovered just behind the goblin. He
didn't notice them because he was
peeking eagerly into the kitchen. A cook,
wearing a white apron, was taking a
tray of delicious-looking chocolate
brownies out of the oven. She put it
down on the kitchen counter and
reached into the oven for a second tray.

The goblin tiptoed into the
kitchen. As Jessica,
Rachel, and Kirsty
watched, he reached
up and stole one of
the fresh-baked
brownies! But he
dropped it
almost
immediately
with a loud
squeal.

"*Ow!*" he
yelped, jumping
up and down, and
blowing on his fingers.
"It's hot!"

The cook whirled around
and frowned at him.

"Well, it serves you right for trying to take a brownie without permission!" she said, putting down the second tray. "Let me check your hand to make sure it isn't burned."

"I don't want you to," the goblin muttered rudely, putting both hands behind his back.

"Don't be silly!" the cook scolded. As the goblin sulkily held out his hand, Jessica

glanced at Rachel and Kirsty in alarm.
"What is she going to think when she sees the goblin has *green* hands?" she whispered. Rachel and Kirsty watched anxiously as the cook stared at the goblin's fingers.

"Why are your hands so dirty and green?" the cook said, frowning. "Have you been rolling around in the grass?"

The goblin shrugged and didn't reply, sticking his bottom lip out grumpily.

"Wash your hands, and then you can have a brownie," the cook instructed him.

"I don't want to wash my hands!" the

goblin said, his face breaking into a sly smile. "But I do want to freeze YOU!"

He jumped forward, touched the cook, and shouted, *"Freeze!"*

Instantly, the cook was frozen solid, and Jessica, Rachel, and Kirsty gasped in horror. The goblin happily began stuffing himself with brownies.

"The poor cook!" Jessica sighed. "Isn't
it lucky that the goblin's magic doesn't
last long? The freezing spell will wear off
soon. At least the cook won't remember
being frozen."

"This could be our chance to grab the
ribbon," Kirsty pointed out. "The
goblin's busy gulping down brownies!"

"You're right," Jessica whispered. "I'll
try to use my magic to untie the ribbon
from his hat."

Rachel and Kirsty nodded, and flew to
hover over the goblin. Jessica
waved her wand, and a
shower of deep pink
sparkles surrounded the
goblin's top hat. As
they did, the ribbon
began to untie itself.

Their hearts pounding, Kirsty and Rachel flew down to grab the jazz ribbon.

"I wonder if there are any more brownies in the oven," the goblin mumbled greedily. He turned around and spotted Rachel and Kirsty reaching toward his top hat.

"*Freeze!*" the goblin yelled, leaping into the air to touch them.

Making a Splash

"Eek!" Kirsty squealed, darting to her left as Rachel dodged to the right. Both girls managed to avoid the goblin's outstretched fingers, but he climbed onto a stool and then onto the kitchen counter to try to reach them.

"Let's get out of here!" Jessica called, whizzing over to the door. Rachel and

Kirsty were quick to follow. As they flew
out the door, they glanced back to see
the goblin firmly re-tying the ribbon to
his hat. Then he jumped off the counter
and dashed after them.

"Now *he's* chasing *us*!" Rachel cried as
they flew down the corridor with the
goblin right behind them.

Jessica led the way out of the house. "Girls, we have to stay away from the goblin or he'll freeze us!" she called as they sped across the garden. "But I *need* to get my ribbon back somehow!"

Kirsty saw the goblin charging out of the house toward them, holding onto his top hat. "Here he comes!" she cried.

Meanwhile, Rachel was staring at the swimming pool up ahead. Suddenly, an idea popped into her head.

"Quick, Jessica, can you make me and Kirsty human-size again?" Rachel asked urgently. "I think there's a way to stop the goblin *and* get the ribbon back!"

Jessica nodded, raised her wand, and showered the girls with sparkles.

Instantly, Rachel and Kirsty shot up to their normal size again. "I'm not scared of you!" the goblin yelled, still rushing toward them. "I can freeze you no matter what size you are!"

"Come on, Kirsty!" Rachel grabbed her friend's hand and pulled her over to the side of the pool. Jessica hovered above them. "When I count to three, jump out of the way!"

The goblin was racing down the path toward the girls, getting closer and closer.

"One," Rachel whispered.

The goblin grinned with glee as he got closer. "You can't escape me now!" he declared.

"Two," Rachel murmured.

The goblin leaped toward the girls and shouted "*Freeze!*" At that moment, Rachel yelled, "THREE!"

Kirsty jumped one way and Rachel jumped the other, but the goblin was going so fast he couldn't stop.

He kept running toward the pool. For
a second he teetered there, on the edge
with a look of horror on his face. But
then he lost his balance and hit the water
with a loud *splash*.

Jessica Jazzes Things Up

"Help!" the goblin sputtered, thrashing around in the pool.

Jessica flew down and sent a stream of sparkling, dark-pink fairy dust toward his top hat. Once again, the magic ribbon untied itself.

"Grab hold of one end," Jessica told the goblin. And then, with a second swirl of

sparkles, she sent the other end of the
ribbon flying through the air toward
Rachel and Kirsty. The girls grabbed
hold of it and pulled the goblin over to

the steps at the side
of the pool. He
crawled out,
grumbling and
shivering, still
clutching his end
of the ribbon.
"This ribbon
doesn't belong to

you," Rachel told him, as she and Kirsty
held on to *their* end just as tightly. "You'd
better give it back!"

The goblin stuck out his tongue.
"No way!" he retorted, still shaking
with cold.

Jessica flew down to join them. "You look cold," she said to the goblin. "How about I make you warm and dry with my magic?"

"Ooh, yes!" the goblin said eagerly.

"Well, if I do, then I want my ribbon in return!" Jessica said firmly, raising her wand and looking questioningly at the goblin. "What do you say?"

The goblin frowned. "But I *like* the ribbon," he grumbled. "And Jack Frost told me to keep it!"

"Oh, but think how nice it would be to be warm and dry!" Kirsty put in. She winked at Rachel and Jessica.

They all knew that goblins *hated* being cold and wet!

The goblin looked uncertain. "It *would* be nice," he agreed slowly.

"And we won't tell Jack Frost you gave us the ribbon," Rachel promised.

The goblin glanced at Jessica. "But can you make me really, *really* warm?"

he asked.

Jessica nodded.
"OK, you can keep the ribbon, then!" the goblin declared, dropping his end of the jazz ribbon. Rachel and Kirsty glanced at each other in delight, and Jessica tapped the

goblin's top hat with her wand. As
sparkling pink fairy dust swirled down
around him, drying him off, the goblin's
face broke into a big smile.

"Ooh, I'm warm all over!" He sighed
happily. "Even my toes are toasty!" He
skipped off happily across the yard.

Rachel and Kirsty let go of the magic
ribbon and it floated over to
Jessica. As it did, it shrank
down to its Fairyland
size. Then it reattached
itself to her wand, and
it glowed an even
deeper, more vivid pink.
"Hooray!" Jessica
cried, stroking her
ribbon as it waved gently in
the evening breeze. "We did it, girls!
Thank you a million times for all
your help!"

Rachel and Kirsty grinned at each
other.

"The party should go well now," Kirsty
pointed out.

"Of course it will!" Jessica declared.
"You go and enjoy yourselves — you
deserve it!" And with a wink, the little
fairy disappeared in a cloud of
pink fairy magic.

The girls hurried back to the tent, but
when they went inside, they were both
disappointed by the scene in front of
them. The music had stopped, some of
the tables and chairs
had been knocked
over, and a
couple of people
were limping
off the dance
floor, shaking
their heads and
looking very sad.

"Oh no!" Rachel groaned. "It looks like the dancing's been a disaster!"

"I think they must have bumped into each other!" Kirsty added, pointing at two people who were sitting on the floor, looking dazed and rubbing their heads.

Suddenly, Rachel spotted Mrs. Tate sitting on one chair with her leg propped

up on another. The two girls quickly ran
over to her.

"Hello, girls," said Mrs. Tate, trying to
smile. "I twisted my ankle when I was
dancing. It's very sore."

"Oh no!" Kirsty cried.

Suddenly, a pink sparkle caught
Rachel's eye. She nudged
Kirsty, and they
glanced up to see
Jessica sitting on
one of the gold
stars hanging
from the ceiling.
Jessica was
waving her wand
back and forth, and the
band began to play again. People looked

at each other nervously, wondering whether to dance again or not.

"Oh!" Mrs. Tate exclaimed, looking surprised. "You know what? I think my ankle stopped hurting!" She swung her leg down to the floor and stood up carefully. "Yes, it feels fine now! Should we go and dance?"

"Oh yes!" Rachel and Kirsty chorused, exchanging a smile as they realized that

Jessica's fairy magic must have healed Mrs. Tate's ankle, too.

The two girls and Kirsty's mom stepped onto the dance floor. People watched nervously at first, but when they realized that nothing was going wrong, they began to join in.

As more people crowded onto the dance floor, Rachel and Kirsty glanced up to see Jessica smiling down at them. Then, with a wave, the little fairy vanished in a swirl of sparkling magic.

"The party's going wonderfully now!" Rachel said.

Kirsty nodded. "And so is the dancing," she said happily. Then she added in a whisper, "Thanks, Jessica!"

THE DANCE FAIRIES

Jessica the Jazz Fairy has
her magic ribbon back. Now Rachel
and Kirsty must help

Serena
the Salsa Fairy!

Join their next adventure in this special
sneak peek!

Fun at the Fiesta

"See you later, Mom," Kirsty Tate said, as she and her best friend, Rachel Walker, got ready to leave the house.

"Four o'clock, in front of the Village Hall," Mrs. Tate reminded the girls. "I should be done with my work by then. I'm sure you'll have a great time at the fiesta. I can't wait to see all the dancing and costumes. Now, girls, promise me that you'll stick together; it's going to be very crowded."

"We will," Kirsty promised. Then, as the two friends headed down the road, she said to Rachel, "Of course we'll stick together. Isn't that when we have all our best adventures?"

Rachel grinned. "I hope we have another one today," she replied.

"The salsa ribbon is still missing," Kirsty said, as they walked toward the center of the village, where the fiesta was taking place. "I wonder if the goblin guarding it will be attracted to the salsa music and turn up at the fiesta today. I hope so."

At that moment, the girls turned the corner onto High Street. For a second, they completely forgot all about goblins as they both took in the sight before them.

High Street looked amazing. Colorful banners and streamers were strung up everywhere, balloons bobbed on the lampposts, and, lining the street, the girls could see tents and booths selling food and drinks. Music was playing, everyone was smiling, and there seemed to be a great buzz of excitement in the air.

"This is so cool!" Rachel said, her eyes shining as she gazed around.

Kirsty grabbed her hand. "Come on," she said eagerly. "Let's go over to the museum, where the parade is going to start. It might be fun to see everyone getting ready."

"OK," Rachel agreed. "And let's keep an eye out for a goblin!"

As they walked toward the museum, they came across a group of friends gathered around a papier-mâché piñata. The piñata was in the shape of a pineapple, and it was dangling from a tree branch. The kids were taking turns putting on a blindfold and whacking the piñata with a stick, hoping to crack it open and release the goodies inside.

"There's Lucy!" Kirsty said, spotting one of her school friends and waving.

Lucy smiled and called them over. "Do you want to take a turn?" she asked.

"Ooh, yes, please," Kirsty said at once, hurrying up to the piñata. Rachel followed and was given the blindfold to tie around her friend's eyes. Then Rachel and Lucy turned Kirsty around three times before putting the stick in her hand.

Dizzy, Kirsty stumbled toward where she thought the piñata was and bashed it with the stick as hard as she could.

Crack! The pineapple split open and lots of candy, small toys, and glitter tumbled to the ground. Everyone cheered and crowded around to gather up the treats.

Rachel was just about to join them when she suddenly noticed a tiny spark of light shoot out of the piñata and up into the air. She knew that it couldn't be a sparkly piece of glitter, because it was flying up and not down.

"That's strange!" Rachel said to herself. Then an exciting thought struck her — could it be a fairy?

RAINBOW magic

THE FUN DAY FAIRIES

Seven Days. Seven Fairies.
Have a Fairy Fun Week!

SCHOLASTIC
www.scholastic.com
www.rainbowmagiconline.com

HiT entertainment

FUNDAY

RAINBOW magic™

SPECIAL EDITION

Three Books in One— More Rainbow Magic Fun!

■ SCHOLASTIC
www.scholastic.com
www.rainbowmagiconline.com

HIT entertainment

RMSPECIAL4

Come flutter by Butterfly Meadow!

#1: Dazzle's First Day

#2: Twinkle Dives In

#3: Three Cheers for Mallow!

#4: Skipper to the Rescue

#5: Dazzle's New Friend

#6: Twinkle and the Busy Bee

#7: Joy's Close Call

#8: Zippy's Tall Tale

#9: Skipper Gets Spooked

SCHOLASTIC

www.scholastic.com

BMEADOW9

MONA the VAMPIRE

The Big Brown Bap Monster

CINAR

Television series © 1999 Fancy Cape Productions Inc.
a subsidiary of CINAR Corporation/Alphanim, France
3, Canal J. All rights reserved.

ORCHARD BOOKS
96 Leonard Street, London EC2A 4XD
Orchard Books Australia
14 Mars Road, Lane Cove, NSW 2066
First published in Great Britain in 1996
This edition published in 2000
ISBN 1-84121-861-8
Text © Hiawyn Oram
Illustrations © Sonia Holleyman
The right of Hiawyn Oram to be identified as the
Author and Sonia Holleyman as the Illustrator of this
Work has been asserted by them in accordance with
the Copyright, Designs and Patents Act, 1988.
A CIP catalogue record for this book is available from
the British Library.
1 3 5 7 9 10 8 6 4 2
Printed in the United Kingdom